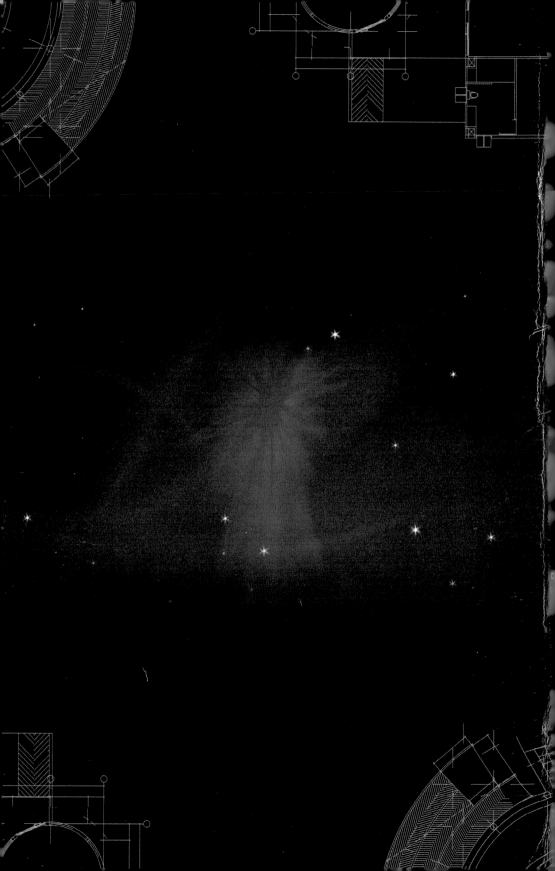

ROBOT RAMPAGE

Steve Barlow and Steve Skidmore

Illustrated by Santy Gutiérrez

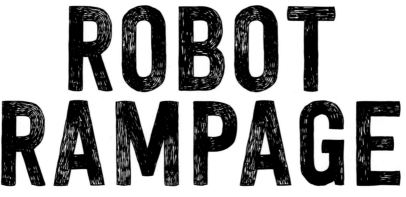

LONDON·SYDNEY

Franklin Watts
First published in Great Britain in 2019 by The Watts Publishing Group

Credits
Series Editor: Adrian Cole
Project Editor: Katie Woolley
Consultant: Jackie Hamley
Designer: Cathryn Gilbert
Illustrations: Santy Gutiérrez
HB ISBN 978 1 4451 5982 9
PB ISBN 978 1 4451 5983 6
Library ebook ISBN 978 1 4451 5984 3

Printed in Dubai.

Franklin Watts
An imprint of
Hachette Children's Group
Part of The Watts Publishing Group
Carmelite House
50 Victoria Embankment
London EC4Y 0DZ

An Hachette UK Company
www.hachette.co.uk

www.franklinwatts.co.uk

THE BADDIES

Lord and
Lady Evil

Dr Y

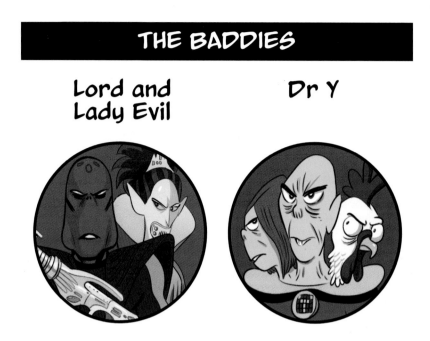

They want to rule the galaxy.

THE GOODIES

Boo Hoo   Jet   Tip

They want to stop them.

"Are they good?" asked Jet.

"I don't know," said Tip. "But they are cheap."

"Let's go!" said Jet.

A three-headed alien met them at the shop. "Hello! Hello! Hello!"

"It's Dr Y!" gasped Tip.

"No! I am his brother, Dr X!" said the alien.

19

"Why does Tee Hee want to kill us?"
said Tip.

"Dr X was really Dr Y!" said Jet.

"I am programmed to kill you," said
Tee Hee.

"Let's get Boo Hoo back!" said Jet.

"It was Dr Y in the shop," said Boo Hoo.

"I got away. Where is Tee Hee?"

"He didn't work out," said Tip.

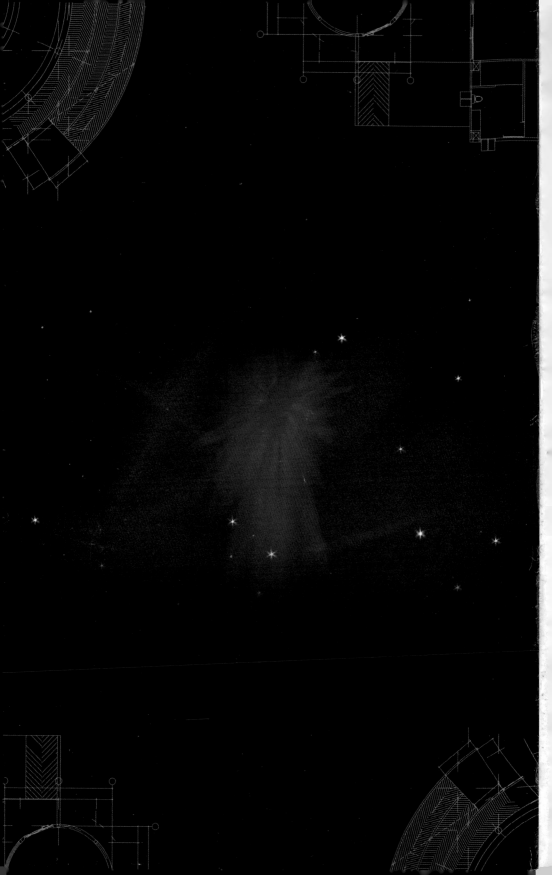